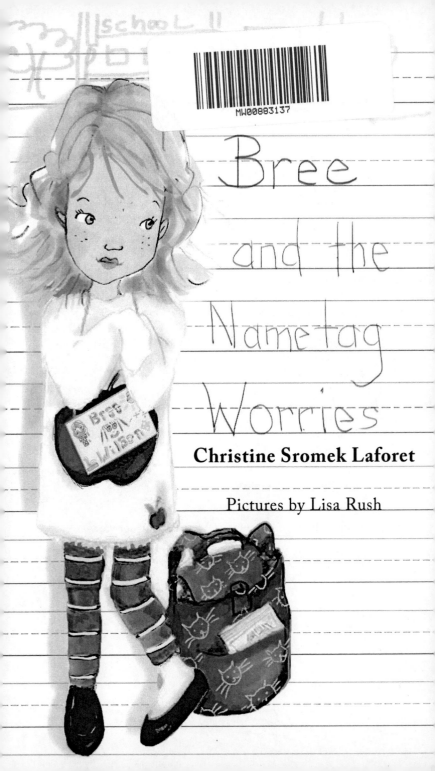

Bree and the Nametag Worries

Christine Sromek Laforet

Pictures by Lisa Rush

Being Bree: Bree and the Name Tag Worries

Summary: Six-year-old Bree Wilson thinks she needs a nametag to make friends on the first day of school. She worries she won't make any since the class is too busy going over rules and reading baby books to share nametags. Belly breaths and counting help Bree calm her worries until her nametag mysteriously disappears at recess and her extra one falls apart. Bree has a meltdown, but, with the help of her Gifted Instruction teacher, she learns friendships are formed with kind words and actions –not just nametags.

Clear Fork Publishing
P.O. Box 870
102 S. Swenson
Stamford, Texas 79553
(325)773-5550
www.clearforkpublishing.com

Printed and Bound in the United States of America.

ISBN - 978-1-946101-26-6
LCN - 2017943940

Clear Fork Publishing

To my family and friends for your support and encouragement – Christine

For my supportive family, Mark, Alexandra and Luke. – Lisa

To Victoria & Anthony,

Happy First Day of School!

Laporte

LET'S MAKE FRIENDS

Use your noodle

Get creative!
Make a nametag
to help your
new friends
learn all
about you.

Be sure to include:
1. Your name.
2. Things you like.
3. A picture of yourself.

Be ready to share your
nametag with your
classmates on the
first day of school.

- Chapter 1 -

The Nametag

If I were a noodle, what kind would I be?

I studied the noodles in my pantry.

Ideas didn't pop into my brain yet. But I kept working on my nametag homework anyway. It was due the first day of school.

I dumped boxes of spaghetti and macaroni on the table. Then I spelled Bree Wilson with the noodles.

Spaghetti pieces made the lines. Macaroni made the curves.

I read my homework paper again.

It was called "Let's Make Friends."

The cook on the page held a plate of noodles. His word bubble said, "Use your noodle."

That's how I knew to use my noodles on my nametag.

The paper said a nametag would help you make friends. And I couldn't live without friends.

Who would listen to my stories and play my made-up games? And what about recess? Who would I do monkey bar contests with?

Plus, only a friend would pick me for teams. I got hit more in dodgeball than a bat at a baseball game, you know.

Friends were more important than air, now that I was a big kid in first grade.

My nametag had to look perfect.

I glued my name on the card my teacher sent. Then I colored the noodles with markers. My name looked like a rainbow.

You also had to make things you liked and add a picture of yourself.

I glued a noodle sun and a noodle ice cream cone with two scoops of strawberry on my nametag. Then I added a book and a plus sign, too.

But my brain felt stuck again. I needed a picture of myself.

A noodle stick girl seemed too easy. I wanted a clever idea.

My brain had to think. My mouth moved side-to-side when I thought.

Brice stopped my brain from working, though. He's my brother.

He dropped his mitt on the table and put his head down. He lost the big game, I think.

I knew what sad felt like.

I felt that way when I sat by myself on the buddy bench at recess.

I could cheer Brice up, though. An idea popped into my brain.

I put a bunch of long spaghetti noodles on my top lip. They stayed right under my nose when I talked.

"I moustache you a question," I said in a low voice. Then I held out a handful of noodles like the cook on my paper. "Should I serve your lunch now? Or should I shave it for later?"

Brice didn't smile.

"Leave me alone," he said.

I moved my lips. My moustache wiggled up and down. My eyes winked all silly-like, too. Then I sneezed.

The spaghetti fell on the floor and broke.

Brice's frown broke, too. He laughed.

"What are you doing with noodles?" he asked.

"It's for my homework," I said. "I made a nametag for the first day of school. Want to see?"

Brice was two hands old. That's four more fingers than me. More fingers meant more practice doing homework.

He looked at my nametag and the homework paper, too. Then he tossed everything on the table.

"You did it wrong," he said all smarty pants-ish.

I felt like a crushed bug.

"But I'm not even done yet," I said.

"Everyone knows the noodle is your brain," Brice said. "You're supposed to think. Not use noodles. The paper tried to be funny."

My moustache was funny. The paper wasn't.

But what if he was right? What if the teacher gave my nametag a big fat X? No one would like me. I'd be the only girl on the planet without any friends.

I'd have to video chat with myself on weekends and play one-kid tag at recess. Who would I invite to my bedroom dance parties? It'd be just me and my stuffies. And stuffies don't even move and shake like a real friend.

Sad feelings spun in my head.

My eyes felt wet. My breaths came fast, too.

But I didn't cry. I stayed in control.

I snapped my fingers to stop those thoughts. Then I took some belly breaths.

Those were the long breaths that went in through my nose and down to my belly. They helped me calm down.

I thought some more about my nametag. My mouth moved side-to-side again, too.

It moved that way when I thought super hard. That's how I knew my special gifts were working.

You couldn't see my gifts. They were in my brain. The doctor said they were in there. I took a test in the summer that proved it.

My brain gifts made me smart and always gave me good ideas.

Right now, they told me to read my homework paper again. I may have missed something before, you know.

I finished reading. Then a smile flashed across my face because I did follow the directions. But I still needed a noodle idea to pop into my brain.

I looked at a macaroni on the table. I picked it up and turned it around.

The frown became a smile. It changed just as fast as my feelings.

That's it!

I was macaroni!

I drew a big macaroni on my nametag. I glued brown spaghetti hair. Then I added a face with blue eyes and eyelashes.

My nametag looked perfect. It's all I needed to make a gazillion new friends.

- Chapter 2 -

The Worries

I plopped on the couch with Mom's cell phone.

Grandma Latski sent me a text.

"Good luck on your first day," she wrote.

I counted two days until school started. But I typed back "THX" anyway.

Grandma bought a new cell phone. She needed practice using it.

I sent her a picture of my nametag.

"2 FIND BFF," I texted. I added a smiley face at the end.

Grandma posted, "I don't understand. I love the nametag and the face, though."

I called her on her real phone and explained things. Then I helped her download an app for the faces.

It took a long time.

"U R A GR8 TEACHER," Grandma texted. She added a face with a wink eye.

I should have a cell phone.

Mom said I wasn't old enough. She said I should be happy to use hers.

I was happy. But I'd be happier if I had my own phone.

Grandma put a face with ZZZs on it. "<3 U. GNITE," she wrote.

I didn't have a good night, though.

I woke up yelling.

Tears wet my face. Blankets tied my legs. Stuffies covered the floor.

Mom rushed to my side. She smoothed my hair and wiped my eyes.

"What if giant ants take my nametag to a picnic?" I asked. "No one will know who I am. Or what if it rains? My pretty, colored noodles would turn into a soggy mess. Then a tornado might come and whip my nametag against my arms and legs. It'd leave yucky colored patches all over my face and skin. I'd look like a zombie. Kids run from zombies, you know."

Mom hugged me. Then we took belly breaths together and counted to ten.

"Are you worried about making friends?" Mom asked.

I sniffled and nodded my head yes.

Mom tucked my stuffies around me. Then she kissed my cheek.

"Let's blow your 'what if' thoughts into a pretend balloon," she said. "Then we'll let it go. All of your worries will float away."

I did those things. But my pretend balloon popped, and my worries dropped right back on top of me.

"What if the kids don't like me?" I asked.

Mom yawned and sat on my bed.

"Of course, they will like you," she said. "You're kind and smart. You like to play and invent fun games. You'll make many new friends."

"But what if no one likes my ideas?" I asked.

"What if no one understands my games? It's hard to talk to kids my age. So, what if I say the wrong things? What if I do something that makes kids laugh at me? What if they call me weird?"

"Your brain works differently than most kids," Mom said. "It puts thoughts together in special ways. That's why you see and feel things in ways other kids may not understand. It's a gift. It makes you, you."

She tapped her finger on my nose when she talked.

"But what if my brain keeps thinking too much?" I asked. "One worry turns into a million more. What if I freak out? What if I lose control and get in trouble? I'll become a troublemaker. And no one EVER wants to be friends with one of those."

"Your feelings are strong," Mom said. "It's part of your gifts. But you know how to calm down. You've practiced all summer."

"But what if school is boring, again?" I asked. "I can already read and solve hard math problems. What if I fall asleep for a hundred years? Kids would pile school papers on me. It'd be so hot when I slept, I'd sweat. Then the papers would stick to my skin. And when I woke up, I'd look like a mummy. I'd probably stink, too. Kids don't like old, stinky mummies."

Mom giggled. "You know your thoughts run wild, sometimes. Don't you?"

I nodded my head yes. Then I laughed at myself, too.

"Don't worry, Bree," Mom said. "This year you'll be in a special class with other kids who have gifts like you. You'll read chapter books and learn many new things. School will be fun and exciting."

"Can you just come with me like last year?" I asked. "You could tell the teacher about me. Plus, I'd feel better if you helped me pick a friend."

I folded my hands like I was praying.

"Please!" I begged.

Mom kissed my cheek and stood to leave.

"You don't need my help making friends," she said. "Once kids get to know you, you'll make your own friends. Your nametag will help."

"How?" I asked.

Mom yawned again. She rubbed her eyes and sat back down on my bed.

"Kids will know your name," she said.

"They will also see some of the things you like. If they like those things, too, you can become friends. Friendship will happen—like magic."

I thought about her words for a while. I pictured a big POOF with stars when I made a friend. There'd be fairies sprinkling sparkle dust, too. I'd laugh and play with my new friend. I'd be the happiest girl alive.

But only if my nametag worked.

"Kids have to like my nametag," I said. "Then they will like me, too. Is that right, Mom?"

She didn't answer.

I called her name three times. Then she said, "Mmmhmm."

"But what about the giant ants and zombie skin?" I asked.

My words sounded silly. But the feelings behind them weren't.

Mom yawned and then talked real slow-like.

"Grandma Latski worried about getting old," she said. "She bought a cell phone and learned to text so she'd feel young. It helped her get rid of her worries. What would help you?"

My brain had to think. My mouth moved side-to-side.

Then I poked Mom until she moved.

"I'll make another nametag," I said. "It'll be a just-in-case one."

"Tomorrow," she said.

Just thinking about that extra nametag calmed my insides.

Next thing you know, the sun shined in

my face.

I spent all day making my just-in-case nametag. It turned out perfect like my real one.

I put it in a plastic baggie in my backpack. Then I picked out my first-day-of-school clothes.

I didn't want the worries to come back.

But guess what?

They came back anyway.

- Chapter 3 -

Stars and Fairies

I put on my apple shirt and a pair of leggings. I picked socks to match my shirt and wore black flats. Then I put the nametag yarn over my head.

I was ready for school, except for one thing. I couldn't eat my breakfast.

The worries bubbled in my tummy.

I tapped my fingers on the table real quick-like. My leg bounced up and down, too.

Brice ate his breakfast.

Mom packed my lunch.

"Did you make me peanut butter and cheese?" I asked.

Cheese made everything taste better, you know.

Mom kissed my head. "I know it's your favorite," she said. Then she poured a cup of coffee and read the news.

"Do you think I'll have someone to eat lunch with?" I asked.

Mom kept reading her tablet. "I'm sure you'll find a new friend," she said.

Brice burped sausage, and the air stunk.

What if my new friend burped tuna fish or pickles? What if the stink fumes melted my nametag?

I plugged my nose.

Brice shoved a huge pancake in his mouth.

A chunk fell out when he chewed. Then he stuffed it right back in.

What if my new friend was gross, too? What if she slobbered or spit on my nametag? It'd be ruined, and I'd NEVER make any friends.

My face felt hot. My breaths came fast.

But I took a belly breath and thought about my new friend.

I pictured a POOF with stars and fairies sprinkling sparkle dust over us. I pictured us laughing at jokes and playing silly games together. I thought only good things until my breaths became regular again.

"I know I'll make a new friend at school," I said. "But who do I sit with on the bus?"

"Sit with Riley," Mom said. "She was in your class last year."

The worries came back. They moved up my throat.

"But that girl has monster feet," I said. "I tripped over those huge things when I showed kids my 100-Day Project. My project box and all one hundred mini-marshmallows ended up as flat as my pancake. What if her feet attack again? What if she stomps all over my nametag?"

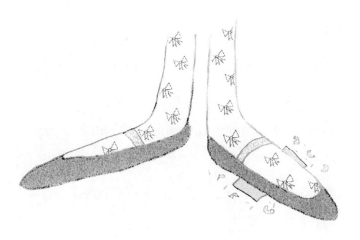

"I'm sure that won't happen," Mom said. "But you made an extra nametag – just in case."

"I can't use it before I even get to school," I said.

"Then sit with someone you don't know," Mom said. "Maybe you'll make a new friend."

"You want me to sit with a stranger?" My words cracked when I talked. My eyes felt wet, too. "You said I shouldn't talk to strangers."

Mom handed me a tissue.

"A bus friend isn't a stranger," she said. "It's someone special to sit with. You can show each other your nametags and become friends."

"But what if she talks a lot?" I asked. "My

ears will hurt from all that talking. But what if she doesn't talk? We'll stare at each other and that will be boring."

My face felt hot. My breaths came fast.

I snapped my fingers a bunch of times to stop those thoughts. Then I took some belly breaths and counted to ten.

Mom did, too.

My insides weren't ready to make friends, yet, I think.

"I'll sit by myself," I said.

"If that will make the worries go away," Mom said.

It did.

I ate my pancake and drank some warm milk. Then I waited for the bus.

Riley sat up front. She tapped the empty spot next to her.

I chose a seat by myself, instead.

I looked out the window and counted houses.

Then a girl with a ponytail and big red bow plopped down next to me.

She wore a blue Ava nametag. She cut out pictures of toys from magazines. She also glued a picture of herself and a dog sitting on some steps.

Those were nice things. Ava must be a nice girl.

My insides felt jumpy since I was about to make a new friend. But the worries moved around in there, too. I didn't want to say the wrong thing, you know.

I smiled the biggest smile ever. Then I held my nametag super close to her eyes so she could see it better.

Ava's head backed away real quick-like.

"Your nametag is very nice," she said.

She liked it! That meant she liked me, too!

My insides felt even more jumpy.

"I used macaroni," I said. "That's a noodle, you know. Remember how the homework paper said to use your noodle? Those were the kind we had in our pantry."

I pointed to a picture on her nametag.

"I like your dog," I said. "He's cute. Did you know canine is another name for a dog? Canines have canine teeth. They're the ones that tear up food. They look like fangs. People have canine teeth, too. I saw pictures of them when I went to the dentist last month. They're pointy. Open your mouth, and I'll show you where yours are."

Ava's eyes grew big. She shook her head no.

Then she poked her head out of the seat and looked all around.

She was looking for the stars and fairies, I think. Those things should be coming now that we were friends, you know.

I kicked my feet and waited for Ava to sit back down.

"You shouldn't kick the seat," she said. "And by the way, your socks don't match."

I pointed to my white shirt and the red apple when I talked.

"One sock is white," I said. "The other one is red. See - they match."

Ava looked at me like I was from Mars.

"What's wrong?" I asked.

"My friend just got on the bus," she said. "I'm sitting with her."

"But I thought we were friends," I said. But Ava left before I finished talking.

I looked out the window the rest of the ride to school.

No one sat with me.

The stars and fairies never came, either.

- Chapter 4 -

Colors

The bus dropped kids off at the school doors.

The first graders walked to the gym.

Mr. Ford stood in front. He was the principal. He told us to look at our nametags.

"If your card is blue, stand by the teacher holding the blue paper," he said.

My nametag color was yellow.

I waited and waited for him to call yellow.

I was good at waiting, you know.

I stood like a statue, except for my eyes. They danced from one basketball hoop to another.

The blue group moved to their classroom. Then the red, green, and purple groups went, too.

Only kids with yellow nametags were left.

Riley was one of them.

We stood behind Mrs. Clark. She held a yellow paper with her name on it.

She was very pretty. I liked her wavy hair and happy eyes.

"Make two lines and follow me," she said.

Riley walked next to me. Her feet looked regular size in those pink glitter shoes.

If she wanted to stomp on my nametag,

she would have worn boots.

There were more nametags in Room 105. They stuck to the desks. That's how I knew where to sit.

I sat between Lauren and Ricky.

Lauren would make a good friend. Her nametag was pretty, even though she didn't use noodles. She made block letters with stripes. She also drew a unicorn.

I liked unicorns, too.

Ricky's mom made his nametag on the computer, I think. It looked very grown-up'ish. It had fancy black letters and pictures of keyboards and controllers.

I didn't like those things. Ricky wasn't friend material.

"We'll share nametags later," Mrs. Clark said. "First, we need to go over the classroom rules."

I listened to the rules as my eyes bopped around the room.

A huge stuffed dog sat in the reading area. Rainbow colors moved across the computer screens. Neon paper, crayons, and markers poked out of pretty baskets.

Everything looked fun and new.

But then, I spotted an alphabet banner. Cartoon animals bent into letters. The number line only counted to twenty. And preschool posters with shapes and colors hung on the wall.

I already knew that baby stuff. I wanted to learn new things.

I took quiet belly breaths. "Just wait," I said in my head. "Things will get better. I'm in the special class."

Then Mrs. Clark talked about the behavior cards. They stuck out of the pocket chart by her desk.

"Everyone begins the day with a green card," she said. "That means you're ready to learn. Let's start with reading."

I liked to read. I learned lots of new things from books.

But we didn't use any!

Mrs. Clark passed out two papers instead.

We cut and folded them into little baby books.

"This will be your story for the week," Mrs. Clark said. "Read it to yourself a few times, if you can. Then color the pictures. I'll call you to read for me at my desk."

I read that story three times.

Do you know what?

It wasn't even a story. It was just a sentence with a color word and a picture.

How could I read that fake book for a whole week? What about the real ones with chapters and one hundred pages?

What if my brain didn't get to learn for another year? It might rot and turn moldy. What if green fuzzy stuff started growing out of my ears?

My face felt hot. My breaths came fast.

I snapped my fingers to stop those thoughts. And guess what?

An idea popped into my brain.

I snapped my fingers two more times and added a foot tap.

Snap-snap-tap. Snap-snap-tap.

I followed that pattern for a while. Then I switched it.

Tap-tap-snap. Tap-tap-snap.

I ended my song with an arm-pumping double-chair scoot.

That's when I bumped Lauren.

She was coloring the ball page.

A streak of orange got out of the lines. The ball looked like it grew a tail.

Lauren flashed mad eyes at me.

They burned my insides. But I couldn't say sorry. Talking broke the rules, you know. I could fix her paper, instead, though.

I'd draw another ball around the orange mark. Then I'd write the letter "s" after the word ball.

The page would say, "See the orange balls."

But before I fixed anything, Lauren's hand shot up.

"That girl hit me!" she told Mrs. Clark. "She ruined my book."

I stood right up and yelled, "No I didn't! I only bumped her."

"But you broke a classroom rule, Bree," Mrs. Clark said. "You didn't keep your hands to yourself. Now please, calm down."

Then she changed my behavior card to yellow.

Yellow was the warning color.

My hands turned into fists and smacked against my legs.

I had to calm down. If I lost control one more time, I'd get the red card. That meant Mrs. Clark would call home.

I'd be punished. Plus, the whole school would stare at that behavior chart and know I was bad. Kids would call me a troublemaker. And troublemakers NEVER had any friends.

My life would be over.

"Calm down," I said to myself. "Relax."

Then I spread my fingers apart and took some belly breaths. I counted in my head while I colored my book.

I reached 1,839 before Mrs. Clark called me to read.

Do you know what?

I read that thing without even looking at it.

- Chapter 5 -

Not Fair

It wasn't fair.

My class didn't show nametags all morning.

We walked around the school and practiced a fire drill instead.

How was I supposed to make friends if no one saw my nametag?

My brain had to think. My mouth moved side-to-side.

Then an idea popped into my brain.

I became a helper.

I held doors open, first.

I was just like a doorman at a fancy hotel. I bowed as kids walked by. But I didn't ask for tips. I put my hand out and showed them my nametag, instead.

Then I passed out papers. I made a pouch out of my shirt and played mailman. I leaned over desks and stood real close to kids when I handed things out. That way my nametag hung right in front of their eyes.

I also collected scraps. I pushed the trashcan while I crawled on the floor. I made garbage truck sounds like CRUSH and BEEP, too. And when I finished cleaning a spot, I reached up and waved my nametag.

No one said they wanted to be my friend, though.

Kids made "tsk" and "ugh" sounds at me, instead.

I even got some eye rolls. Eye rolls were never a good thing.

The worries moved in my tummy. It grumbled down there, too, since it was almost lunchtime.

I still didn't have anyone to eat with. But guess what?

Another idea popped into my brain.

I made throat noises.

Lauren would have to look at me, now. I'd move my mouth and tell her I was sorry about things.

I couldn't poke her or use my voice. I didn't want to break a rule and get the red card, you know.

But Lauren kept her back to me. And I felt like a crushed bug, again.

I raised my hand.

"Can we please show nametags?" I asked Mrs. Clark. "I want to make friends before lunch and recess."

"That's a good idea," Mrs. Clark said. "We'll go in ABC order."

I didn't see any A names when I was a helper. That meant B, for Bree, started.

I pushed in my chair and walked to the front of the room.

"We go by last names when we use ABC order," Mrs. Clark said.

Wilson started with W. W was at the end of the alphabet. That meant I was one of the last kids.

"That's not fair!" I said. "It was my idea. I should go first."

Then my feet stomped all by themselves.

Mrs. Clark headed for the behavior chart.

Do you know what?

The stomping stopped super quick. I plopped in my seat and folded my hands like an angel.

I was good at waiting.

Mrs. Clark called Lily first.

Lily drew herself and a pony on her nametag. She liked pony books and pony dress-up toys.

I don't think Lily and I would get along very well, though.

Ponies were boring. I liked unicorns better. Plus, Lily drew all of her pictures, and you were supposed to use noodles.

Tyler didn't use noodles either. He used basketball stickers and a picture of himself on a sports card. He talked about basketball camp and did a pretend shot. Then he showed us some other basketball moves. He was a fun boy, even though he didn't follow the nametag directions.

Ricky talked a lot when it was his turn. He liked computers and video games. He said he made his nametag all by himself. Instead of noodles, he used pictures called clip-art and fancy letters called Candy Round font.

Do you know what?

No one used noodles on their nametag.

Mrs. Clark didn't give anyone a big fat X, either. She just tapped her fingers and looked at the clock when Ricky answered video game questions.

She was waiting for someone to show her a noodle nametag, I think.

But she wouldn't wait much longer.

It was my turn next. I knew it because our desks went in ABC order by our last names.

Kids had to look at my nametag now. I rushed things before, I think.

I sat super straight and folded my hands tight. I waited for Mrs. Clark to call my name.

"Line up for lunch and recess," Mrs. Clark said. "We'll finish when we get back."

My insides cried. My bottom lip stuck out, and I sniffled, too.

"I'm good at waiting. I'm good at waiting," I said a zillion times in my head. I closed my eyes and pictured a bunch of friends standing around me.

I took a belly breath and searched for my lunch in my backpack. Then I hung my head and moved like a snail all the way to the lunchroom.

Riley tapped me. "You forgot to take off your nametag," she said.

My whole body shook.

If something happened to my nametag, I'd spend the rest of my life all alone.

I marched right up to the lunch lady who opened water bottles. I pulled her apron string until she looked.

Then I asked her if I could take my nametag back to my classroom.

She said, "No. Go back to your seat."

"But . . . But . . ." My mouth didn't work. My feet didn't either.

I stared at the air in front of my face.

Riley led me back to our class table.

"Mrs. Clark said to sit here," she said.

I sat at the end of the long table by Riley and Lily.

No one talked, though. Lunchtime was only for eating.

So, guess what?

I didn't need a lunch friend after all. But I still needed my nametag to make friends in class.

I tucked it in my shirt and didn't eat.

After lunch, I tossed my lunch bag in the class bin. I ran to the tallest slide. Then I hung my nametag on the ladder by the top step.

It would stay safe up there.

- Chapter 6 -

Recess Problem

I had a problem.

I didn't make any friends before recess because I didn't show my nametag. I couldn't make friends now because my nametag needed to stay safe. So, what should I do until recess was over?

My brain had to think. My mouth moved side-to-side.

I decided to play.

I didn't like strangers. But I spotted Riley.

She played Four-Square with some girls. Those girls weren't really strangers because they knew Riley.

I joined Riley in the Ace spot. Then I caught the ball.

"What are you doing?" Riley asked. "This is my square."

"I'm playing with you," I said.

"Give us the ball back," the girl with curly hair said.

"I have a new game," I said. "I call it Animal Pop. You throw the ball in the air. Then you say the name of an animal when you clap. Plus, you have to go in ABC order. I'll start."

I threw the ball in the air and clapped

once.

"Alligator," I said.

I caught the ball and bounced it to the girl with curly hair in the Jack square.

"You say alligator and an animal that begins with the letter B while you clap two times," I said.

"I'm not playing that game," the girl with curly hair said. "It's too hard. It's not even your turn to pick."

"Can I have a do-over?" Riley asked.

All the girls nodded their heads yes.

"Get off the court," the girl with curly hair said. "You have to wait in line."

I waited in line. But no one played hand-slapping games with me when I clapped. No one even looked at me when I made silly faces.

I felt like a ghost.

Then I made spooky sounds and pretended to float.

I floated by the girls waiting to play and shouted, "BOO!"

They didn't play ghost back. They left the line, instead.

I floated by the girls in the squares and scared them, too.

"Cut it out!" the girl with curly hair yelled. "Stop being a troublemaker. Wait in line for your turn."

I wasn't a troublemaker. I was only playing.

Then I showed that girl my spooky face.

"You're weird," she said.

She didn't understand my game. Her words hurt, though.

I wanted to stomp and scream and call her a big meanie. But I was a ghost. And ghosts only said BOO.

I yelled, "BOOOOOO!!" until all those bad feelings inside of me went away.

Then I floated around the playground until I found someone else I knew.

Lauren and Lily played jump rope.

Lauren jumped while Lily and a girl in a flower dress twirled.

Lauren tried to jump in. But she waited too long and missed.

I was good at jumping rope. So, I stopped being a ghost. And when the rope twirled again, I jumped in.

Lauren stomped her foot and made a hmph sound.

"No cuts," she said.

The rope stopped twirling.

"What are you doing?" the flower girl asked.

"Keep going," I said. "I'm showing Lauren how to jump in. I'm a good teacher, you know."

"I don't want your help," Lauren said. "You ruined my book."

"I'm sorry a million times," I said.

"Go away," the flower girl yelled. "I'm playing with Lauren and Lily."

Lily stood next to me.

"Bree is in our class," she said. "We can all play together."

"If her name is Bree, then she can't play with us," the flower girl said. "She's not part of our club."

A club meant you had friends. You only played with other kids in your club. You had rules and special hand signs. And best of all, club kids liked the same things.

"Is it the Jump Rope Club?" I asked. "Can I be in it, too?"

"Sorry, Bree," Lauren said all meanie-like. "It's the L-Club. Your name has to start with the letter L. There's Lily, Leah, and me. Your name starts with a B. So, you can't be in our club."

The worries flip-flopped in my tummy.

What if everyone else already had clubs? What if those club kids made a rule to ship me to an island because I was the only one without a club? I'd be in a school all by myself. I'd float my homework back in bottles. But who would I write notes to?

I didn't even make a friend, yet, to read them.

"But . . . But . . ." I started to say. "I could change my name."

Lauren and Leah shouted, "NO!" Then they made the letter L out of their fingers.

"You're a troublemaker, Bree," Lauren said. "And we don't play with troublemakers."

"I'm not a troublemaker," I said. "I didn't get the red card. You just don't know me, yet. I didn't show my nametag the right way."

Lauren rolled her eyes.

"Maybe we could play tomorrow," Lily said.

But I wanted to play today.

I grabbed the jump rope and yelled, "Try and catch me!"

Then I ran on the grassy hill. I raced to the

swings and hid by the monkey bars to rest.

The L-Club girls found me. They brought the recess lady with them, too.

She blew her whistle.

"Why did you take the jump rope?" she asked. "It doesn't belong to you."

"We were playing," I said.

Those L-Club girls shook their heads no.

"Give it back," the recess lady said. "Then stay on The Wall until you're ready to behave."

I gulped.

"But . . . But . . . That's where the troublemakers stand," I said.

The recess lady nodded her head yes.

I watched my feet move to that brick wall.

I wasn't a troublemaker. But what if kids saw me? What if no one wanted to be friends with me now?

I dropped to the ground and curled up to hide my face.

I became a ball . . . or an egg.

The Humpty Dumpty rhyme popped in my brain. He was stuck on a wall, too, you know.

I wobbled back and forth and side-to-side. Then I fell over and cracked.

That's when I saw her.

And she was staring.

- Chapter 7 -

Squiggles

I stared back at the girl who stared at me first.

She had squiggles everywhere.

Her dark hair was squiggles. Squiggle ribbon twisted around her hair ties. More squiggles stuck to her sandals. There were even colored squiggles stuck on her cake shirt.

She put her hand by her mouth like she was making whispers in someone's ear.

I didn't see anyone, though.

I walked up to that girl and asked, "What are you doing?"

"Maddie wants to know if you want to play," she said.

I looked around.

"Who's Maddie?" I asked.

"My friend," the squiggle girl said. "She's right here."

"I don't see anyone."

"I know," she said.

Then I understood the squiggle girl's game. I smiled because I liked playing make-believe, too.

"Hi, Maddie," I said to the make-believe girl. "It's nice to meet you. I like your cell phone. Can I use it?"

I pretended to take it.

I took a selfie and sent it to Grandma Latski.

"My Grandma Latski got a new cell phone," I told Maddie. "I had to teach her how to text."

I handed it back to her. "Thanks," I said.

"Do you have a real cell phone?" the squiggle girl asked.

"No," I said. "But I want one."

"Me, too," she said. "But my mom said I wasn't old enough."

"Me, too!" I yelled all excited-like. I even jumped up and down.

Then the squiggle girl looked at my feet.

"Why don't your socks match?" she asked.

I took a belly breath and explained things.

Then I waited for her to say something mean.

She didn't. She smiled, instead.

"That's so cool!" the squiggle girl said. "I wish my mom would let me do that."

"My mom never says anything," I said. "She's too busy making sure I brush my hair and my teeth. She doesn't even look at my feet."

Then, with my finger, I told the squiggle girl to come closer. I had a secret to whisper in her ear.

"You have to put the extra two socks in the laundry basket, too," I said. "That way your socks are even. They match up when your mom is folding."

"You're so smart," the squiggle girl said. "I bet you know the alphabet song. Want to sing it?"

My face scrunched into a frown because that was a boring, baby song.

"You know it backwards, right?" the squiggle girl added.

I made a smiley face.

"That's the only way I'll sing it," I said. "Does Maddie sing, too?"

The squiggle girl laughed.

"Maddie went home," she said. "She only plays with me when I'm alone."

I laughed, too.

Then I sang songs with the squiggle girl. We pushed each other on the swings. We even played hand-slapping games.

"Guess what?" the squiggle girl asked.

"What?"

"Today's my birthday," she said.

I sang her the Happy Birthday song.

"Is that why you're wearing all those squiggles?" I asked.

"Yep!" she said. "I wanted to look like a birthday present. Watch this."

She pulled the squiggle ribbon on her hair tie. It was long and straight. Then she let it go, and it popped back into a squiggle.

"Want to try?" she asked.

I nodded my head yes. Then I pulled the squiggle ribbon and laughed.

"Your name should be Squiggles," I said.

"Yes!" Squiggles shouted. "That's a fun nickname. You should see all the squiggles I put on my nametag. I tried to make it look like a birthday party. I drew a cake and even made special party hats. I left it in my classroom, though."

"I put mine on the playground," I said. "Want to see it?"

Squiggles nodded her head yes.

We held hands and skipped to the slide.

I climbed the ladder. But when I got to the top, my nametag was gone.

- Chapter 8 -

The Mystery – Part 1

"Where's my nametag?" I yelled.

My face felt hot. My breaths came fast.

How could Squiggles be my friend? My nametag was gone.

"Quit holding up the line," some boy at the bottom of the slide hollered.

"You be quiet, Mister!" Squiggles yelled. "We have a problem up here."

Then she tapped my arm and said, "Don't worry. I'll help you find it. It'll be okay."

I did belly breaths all the way down the slide.

My just-in-case nametag was in my backpack. I could still make friends in class. But I liked Squiggles. I wanted her for my friend. I wanted to see the fairies sprinkling sparkle dust with her.

"Your nametag is missing," Squiggles said. "This is a mystery. I've read all about them. I've always wanted to solve one, too."

"We can be like that guy Sherlock Holmes," I said. "We can even talk funny. What should we do first?"

"We ask questions and take notes," Squiggles said in a funny voice. She looked through a pretend magnifying glass. "Then we search for clues."

I pulled a pretend notebook from my sock and a pretend pencil from Squiggles' hair. Then I handed them to Squiggles.

"What does your nametag look like?" Squiggles asked.

"I spelled my name with noodles," I said. "I also drew a macaroni face."

Squiggles wrote those words on the pretend paper.

"Where did you leave it?" she asked.

"On the tallest slide," I said. "It was on the top part of the ladder."

"Are you sure this was the slide?"

I nodded my head yes.

We searched for clues by the slide and the ladder. We even dug through the mulch and dirt.

"I found one!" I yelled. I picked up a macaroni and showed it to Squiggles.

She studied the clue.

"Let's look for another one," she said. "We need to follow the trail. It will lead us to your nametag."

Kids watched us poke the ground.

"What are you doing?" someone asked.

I explained things.

Then Squiggles asked them if they saw my nametag.

Kids said, "No." But she wrote notes in her pretend notebook anyway.

Then Squiggles told them to ask their friends, too.

Do you know what?

Everyone talked about my missing nametag. Kids I didn't even know searched the playground. They all wanted to help.

Kids ran up to me and asked questions. One girl even said I could use her nametag.

Then Tyler, from my class, put two pink macaroni and a yellow one in my hand.

"I found these clues over there," he said. He pointed between the jump rope spot and the Four-Square court.

Guess what?

I knew who took my nametag.

- Chapter 9 -

The Mystery – Part 2

I pointed across the playground.

"One of those meanie girls took my nametag!" I yelled.

"You can't blame kids without proof," Squiggles said. "We'll ask questions first. I'll talk. You watch and take notes. Look for blinks. People blink a lot when they don't tell the truth.

I learned that trick from a book."

Then she handed me the pretend notebook.

We found the L-Club girls on the black top. They still jumped rope.

"Did any of you go on the slide today?" Squiggles asked.

I watched each girl say, "No."

They blinked regular blinks. They didn't take my nametag.

Then Lauren and Leah took the jump rope and walked away.

"What happened at the slide?" Lily asked.

Squiggles pointed to me. "Someone took her nametag," she said. "It was on the slide. We found some clues. Now we're here."

"I didn't see it," Lily said. "But I'll help you look."

I smiled at Lily. She was a nice girl, even

though she liked horses and was part of the L-Club.

I looked at my pretend list.

"We should go to the Four-Square court next," I said.

The Four-Square girls stopped playing their game.

The girl with curly hair caught the ball. "Did you find the missing nametag yet?" she asked.

I shook my head no.

Then Riley patted my arm. "I'm sorry," she said. "We looked all over the black top. But we couldn't find it."

"We could look somewhere else," the girl with curly hair said. "Tell us where to go."

"How about by the slide?" Squiggles asked. "Have any of you been there today?"

It was a trick question.

But all the girls said, "No." And no one blinked a lot.

"I'll look there," Riley said. Then she ran to the slide.

"We'll look by the hill," the girl with curly hair said. She ran off with the rest of the Four-Square girls.

I felt very surprised that those meanie girls weren't acting mean anymore. Squiggles was right. Talking worked.

We hunted for my nametag some more.

I found another macaroni clue by the recess door.

"We know your nametag is falling apart," Squiggles said. "But who took it? And where is it now?"

Then Riley brought us a boy with a scratch

on his nose.

"He saw your nametag on the slide," she said.

The boy nodded his head yes.

"It was hanging on the ladder," he said. "There was a big macaroni face. I think there was a macaroni ice cream cone on it, too."

"Yes! That's it!" I yelled.

"Do you know what happened to it?" Squiggles asked.

The boy shook his head no.

"I fell at the bottom of the slide," he said. "Then I went to the nurse. It was gone by the time I went up the slide again."

"That's not really a clue," Squiggles said.

"I think I know who took it, though," the boy said.

We all got jumpy because we almost solved the mystery.

"It was a bird," the boy said. "It could use the macaroni for food and the yarn for a nest. Plus, I saw a bunch of them flying around. That's why I fell. One of them tried to poke my eye out."

"Birds!" Squiggles and I both yelled together.

We pointed to a big bunch of them. They flew by the picnic tables.

"Over there!" Squiggles shouted. Then she took off.

She was a fast runner.

But before I got to the tables, the recess bell rang.

Everyone stopped playing and lined up by their color cards.

It was time to go back to class. But did we solve the mystery?

I stood in my yellow line and looked all around for Squiggles. I couldn't see her anywhere.

The worries bubbled in my tummy.

If I brought my just-in-case nametag to recess tomorrow, we could still be friends. But what if a storm flooded the playground?

It'd be under water. What if Squiggles couldn't swim? What if I NEVER saw her again? I didn't even know her real name.

I grabbed my lunch bag from the bin and took belly breaths all the way down the hall.

- Chapter 10 -

The Worst Day Ever

My tummy grumbled all the way to Room 105.

The worries bounced around in there too, since I didn't know if I'd ever see Squiggles again.

My feet stopped in front of my backpack. It was on a hook near the classroom door.

I patted the side of it.

At least I could still make friends in class.

I super quick opened my lunch bag, ate half my sandwich, and grabbed my just-in-case-nametag.

But then I gulped the biggest gulp ever.

Scoops of strawberry were missing. The curves around the B and one of the e's fell off, too.

Why didn't I make a just-in-case nametag for my just-in-case nametag?

Kids couldn't tell what I liked anymore. They couldn't even read my name.

No one would like it. They wouldn't like me, either!

Now I'd NEVER make any friends.

It was the worst day ever!

Mrs. Clark stepped into the hall.

"Hurry up, Bree," she said. "It's your turn to share."

I needed to fix my nametag. But I didn't have any glue!

Then an idea popped into my brain.

I picked the loose macaroni out of the baggie and wiped them in the leftover sandwich peanut butter. Then I stuck the macaroni back on my nametag and put the yarn over my head.

I took a belly breath and stood in front of the class.

"My name is Bree Wilson," I said. "And this is my nametag."

I pointed my fingers at it and smiled real big, too. Then I waited for kids to say how much they liked summer and ice cream.

No one said anything, though. So, I tried harder to make kids like me.

I acted like a TV star. I wiggled my hips when I walked up and down the desk rows. Then I struck a pose and modeled my nametag some more.

But no one said they liked books or solving math problems. Or even that they were creative like me.

I was in a special class this year. Kids were supposed to understand me.

Why wasn't my nametag working? Why didn't anyone want to be my friend?

Ricky raised his hand.

"I thought you lost your nametag," he said.

"I know what happened!" Riley yelled out. "I was with her. Birds took it."

Do you know what?

Everyone talked about the birds. But they should have talked about me!

And then the worst thing ever happened.

The peanut butter stopped sticking!

At first, only Lauren knew.

She pointed and giggled when a noodle fell off. Then she whispered to the other kids to watch too.

Tih-tih tah. Tih-tih-tah.

Some pieces bounced under desks and chairs. Others ended up on the reading rug. One piece even bounced off a crayon and landed on Mrs. Clark's shoe!

The whole class laughed at me.

Mrs. Clark clapped her hands, and kids quieted down.

But my face felt hot. And my breaths came fast.

Then a boy named Tate raised his hand.

"Why did you use macaroni?" he asked.

Before I even moved my mouth, Lily shouted back, "Maybe it's her favorite food!"

My hands clenched into fists. I shook my head no.

"Then why didn't you use crayons and glue like everyone else?" Tate asked. "And what's all that brown smeary stuff?"

"It's mud!" Lauren answered.

Kids bent over laughing. They slapped their legs and banged on desks. Tyler even snorted before he fell off his chair.

I held my breath to keep my mad feelings inside.

Then Lauren said, "Did you see her macaroni face? That girl is sooo weird."

"I AM NOT WEIRD!" I yelled. Then

I ripped that stupid nametag off my neck
and stomped all over it.

It didn't help me make any friends!

Everyone stopped and stared.

I took some belly breaths. Then I looked
at the floor.

I said, "Sorry," and threw the nametag
pieces away.

But Mrs. Clark changed my behavior card
to red.

Then she called home.

Mom told me to use my calm down steps.

It was too late, though.

I was a troublemaker. My whole class knew
it. Now I'd NEVER make any friends.

Were troublemakers even allowed to stay
in school?

I put my head on my desk while kids

finished showing nametags.

Then a man with a bald head knocked on the door.

"Bree Wilson," he said. "Come with me."

- Chapter ll -

The GI's

I gulped and took baby steps towards the man with the bald head.

Did he take troublemakers away? Where did he take them?

He called Lily, Ricky, and Tate, too.

Tate was on the red card, like me. He couldn't stop talking. But Lily and Ricky didn't do anything wrong.

"I'm Mr. Gunner," the man with the bald head said. "You little GI's follow me."

"GI's are soldiers," Tate said. His body stiffened, and he did a salute. "I have a GI Joe at home."

Did troublemakers go to the army?

I couldn't march fifty miles or do push-ups. What if the army food made me puke? I didn't even like the color green!

The worries flipped and flopped in my tummy. They twisted and turned and tied into knots.

Lily tapped Mr. Gunner's arm.

"You took my sister last year," she said.

Was Lily's sister a troublemaker? Did Lily wait a whole year to visit her? Was Ricky visiting a troublemaker, too.

No one would visit me. I didn't have any friends. What if Brice never even missed me? I'd be all alone in the army - forever. And it was all because of my nametag!

The worries burst out of me.

I grabbed Mr. Gunner's leg.

"Don't take me to the army!" I cried. "I don't want to be a little GI! I don't want to fight bad guys. I want to make friends. I promise I'll behave. Give me another chance. PLEASE!"

Lily, Ricky, and Tate stopped moving.

Mr. Gunner knelt down. He patted my hands.

"We're not going to the army," he said. "I'm taking you to Room 136."

I sniffled.

"Is that where the troublemakers go?" I asked.

Mr. Gunner shook his head no.

"It's Mrs. Olsen's class," he said. "She's your afternoon teacher. All of you are in a special class. It's called Gifted Instruction. That's why I call you GI's."

My brain had to think. My mouth moved side-to-side.

I understood things.

G stood for Gifted. I stood for Instruction. My special class wasn't with Mrs. Clark. It was with Mrs. Olsen.

That meant Lily, Ricky, and Tate had gifts, like me.

I wiped my eyes in my apple shirt. My breaths became regular again, too.

Lily held my hand. She tried to make me feel better, I think.

We walked down the hall together.

Then Ricky asked Tate if he could play after school.

Tate said yes.

I turned around and looked at that boy.

"You're not allowed," I said.

"Why not?"

"Only friends play together," I said. "And you can't have any. You got the red card. That means you're a troublemaker. Troublemakers DON'T have any friends."

"I can have as many friends as I want," Tate said. "And I'm not a troublemaker. I didn't do those bad things on purpose. They were just mistakes. Sometimes I can't control myself."

Sometimes I couldn't control myself, either. I made some mistakes, today, too.

But if Tate wasn't a troublemaker, then I wasn't one either. Maybe I could still make friends in my special class.

Except that I couldn't.

I didn't have a nametag, and I needed one to make friends.

We stopped outside Room 136.

"Make sure you show Mrs. Olsen your nametag," Mr. Gunner said.

I sniffled, and my eyes felt wet again. I pulled the bottom of Mr. Gunner's shirt.

"My nametag is gone," I said.

Mr. Gunner smiled. "Don't worry, Bree," he said. "Everything will be fine."

I wanted to believe him. But the worries wouldn't let me.

- Chapter 12 -

Room 136

"Welcome to Room 136," a grandma-like lady with glasses said. "My name is Mrs. Olsen. I'm your GI teacher. Roam around the room and make friends. We'll share nametags in a little bit."

Lily, Ricky, and Tate left.

My feet didn't move, though.

My face felt hot. My breaths came fast.

But the screams weren't coming this time. Tears were.

They dripped down my cheek.

Mrs. Olsen bent down so her eyes were right in front of mine. Then she took my hands in hers. We did belly breaths together.

"Why are you sad?" she asked.

I sniffled. "I don't have a nametag," I said. "I can't make any friends."

Mrs. Olsen handed me a tissue.

"What happened to yours?" she asked.

I explained things.

"Your nametag was very important to you," Mrs. Olsen said. "But try to make friends without one." Then she welcomed another group of kids.

I still didn't know how to make friends. But my feet moved around the room anyway.

I watched Lily play with a girl who wore a pink headband. Her nametag said Emma.

They spelled words with letter tiles.

Then another girl sat at the table with them. Her name was Kate. She held a stuffed kitty. There was also a kitty on her nametag.

"I have that game at home," Kate said. "You're not playing it right."

Then the kitty messed up all the tiles.

Lily and Emma moved to the reading area.

Kate played by herself. She didn't make any friends. It didn't even matter that she wore a nametag. She was bossy. She ruined the game. She should have asked to play something new first.

My brain started to think.

Was I bossy, too?

My feet walked to the back of the room.

The boy with a scratch on his nose played on a computer. He slapped the screen with his Quinn nametag.

Ricky joined him. "Want some help?" he asked. "I'm good at computers."

Quinn nodded his head yes.

Ricky explained things. He watched and waited while Quinn typed on the keyboard.

Then POOF!

It happened.

They were friends.

I didn't see any stars or fairies sprinkling sparkle dust. But the boys talked and played computer games. They high-fived each other and laughed.

Ricky didn't use his nametag. He didn't do anything fancy, either. He just talked and acted nice. He was himself, I think.

Was that how you made friends?

The only time I acted regular was with Squiggles. We talked, laughed, and played. She even helped me look for my missing nametag.

Do you know what?

Squiggles *was* my friend.

You can't see the friendship magic. You feel it.

Squiggles and I *did* all the friend things together. It didn't matter if she saw my nametag or not. It was more important to talk and be myself.

My nametag only told a little bit about me. What I did told more.

I made a big sigh, though. Would I ever see Squiggles again?

Then someone tapped my back.

Guess what?

It was Squiggles!

"You're a GI, too?" she asked.

I nodded my head yes.

We smiled the biggest smiles ever and hugged each other tight.

It was the best day ever!

"Sorry I didn't solve the mystery," Squiggles said. "Your nametag wasn't by the birds. But do you like mine? I wrote my name in cursive."

I couldn't read those loopy letters.

"It's very pretty," I said. "It's all squiggly just like a party."

Then I sang her the Happy Birthday song again.

A boy with spiky hair named Curtis, sang, too. He added the part with the monkey.

"It's Smelly-Belly's birthday," he told some other kids.

Squiggles folded her arms and stomped. "Kids called me that last year," she said. "Now they're going to call me Smelly-Belly again. I don't like the name Belle. It rhymes with too many words."

I smiled on the inside because I finally knew Squiggles' real name. But on the outside, my face didn't smile because Squiggles felt mad.

I patted her back. "It's okay," I said.

Then I showed her how to take belly breaths.

"Tell kids to call you Squiggles," I said. "Explain things when you show your nametag."

"What are you going to do when it's your turn?" Squiggles asked. "We never found yours."

My brain had to think. My mouth moved side-to-side.

"I'm going to explain things, too," I said. "Using words helps you solve problems. It also helps you make friends."

I sat with my new friend, Squiggles, on the reading rug. We flipped through books with chapters and one hundred pages. We looked at the puzzles and thinking games on the shelf. We even peeked in the craft closet and talked about projects we could make.

Then it was time for nametags.

Squiggles went first, and everyone liked her new nickname.

I took a belly breath when it was my turn.

"Hi," I said. "My name is Bree Wilson. I like summer and ice cream and rainbow colors. I can already read. And I like math. I glued noodles on my nametag. And I'm sad that it's gone, now."

"I know you," Grace said. "I looked for your nametag by the slide."

"I looked by the swings," Kaylee said. "I'm sorry you didn't find it. It sounded very pretty."

"Thanks," I said. I smiled, too, because those girls helped me. And that's what friends did.

Do you know what?

My nametag helped me make friends after all. It just didn't help like I thought.

Then Malcolm stood up. He pushed in his chair and fixed his bow tie before he talked.

"I know that brie is a kind of cheese," he said. "You spell it, b-r-i-e. Do you spell your name that way?"

"It's spelled B-r-e-e," I said.

He nodded his head and sat back down.

"Did you use macaroni because you like cheese?" Quinn asked. "Robins like cheese, too. Those are the birds that live by my house. We feed them cheddar."

"I like that kind, too," I said. "Cheese is my favorite food. But that's not why I used macaroni."

Then I explained about the cook on the homework paper and my feelings.

"I get it!" Tate shouted. "You used both noodles. The thinking kind and real ones."

"That was a smart idea," Grace said. "I bet it was fun making your nametag."

"I should have used rotini noodles on mine," Squiggles said. "They would have matched my hair."

Those nice words made me feel happier than unicorns eating jellybeans.

Then Mr. Gunner walked in the room. He held something in his hand.

"This was in the office," he said. "I think it belongs to you."

It was my nametag!

The sticky note on the back said, "From Ava."

Ava found my nametag at recess. She knew it was important. She took it to the office. Maybe she'd be a good bus friend after all.

I showed everyone my nametag. But I didn't need it anymore. I had already made a roomful of new friends.

Being Bree Book 2

Bree and the Loose Tooth Worries

Coming early 2018!

– How to Take a Belly Breath –

1. Take a long, deep breath in through your nose
2. Hold it inside and count to three in your head
3. Blow the air slowly out of your mouth like you're blowing a bubble

Calming Down Steps

STOP – when your feelings start to spin out of control, do an action to stop those thoughts

NAME YOUR FEELING – it makes you think before you act

CALM DOWN – take deep breaths, count, or use positive self-talk

For more information visit:
Grade 1 Second Step Program Scope and Sequence, Unit 3: Emotion Management, Lessons 12–16, www.secondstep.org

Christine Sromek Laforet
Author

Chris received her M.A.Ed. from Baldwin-Wallace University and taught in the Cleveland area before raising a family. She is a member of the Society of Children's Book Writers and Illustrators and is involved in many local critique groups. She resides in Avon, Ohio with her husband, three children, and two crazy dogs.

Lisa Rush
Illustrator

Lisa Rush is a Children's Book Illustrator. She grew up in Canada and has lived in four different countries and five different states, and now lives in upstate NY with her husband, two children, two Labrador retrievers and a fish her son named Blue Whale.

CPSIA information can be obtained
at www.ICGtesting.com
Printed in the USA
LVOW08s1137210717
542149LV00002B/169/P

9 781946 101266